CHILD OF THE SUN

CHILD OF THE SUN

by Leigh Brackett

Far beyond molten Mercury flashed the Patrol-pursued Falcon....Out to where black Vulcan whirled his hidden orbit, and a flame-auraed last child of Sol played his cosmic game.

*

Eric Falken stood utterly still, staring down at his leashed and helpless hands on the controls of the spaceship *Falcon*.

The red lights on his indicator panel showed Hiltonist ships in a three-dimensional half-moon, above, behind, and below him. Pincer jaws, closing fast.

The animal instinct of escape prodded him, but he couldn't obey. He had fuel enough for one last burst of speed. But there was no way through that ring of ships. Tractor-beams, criss-crossing between them, would net the *Falcon* like a fish.

There was no way out ahead, either. Mercury was there, harsh and bitter in the naked blaze of the sun. The ships of Gantry Hilton, President of the Federation of Worlds, inventor of the Psycho-Adjuster, and ruler of men's souls, were herding him down to a landing at the lonely Spaceguard outpost.

A landing he couldn't dodge. And then....

For Paul Avery, a choice of death or Happiness. For himself and Sheila Moore, there was no choice. It was death.

The red lights blurred before Falken's eyes. The throb of the plates under his feet faded into distance. He'd stood at the controls for four chronometer days, ever since the Hiltonists had chased him up from Losangles, back on Earth.

He knew it was because he was exhausted that he couldn't think, or stop the nightmare of the past days from tramping through his brain, hammering the incessant question at him. *How?*

How had the Hiltonists traced him back from New York? Paul Avery, the Unregenerate recruit he went to get, had passed a rigid psycho-search—which, incidentally, revealed the finest brain ever to come to the Unregenerate cause. He couldn't be a spy. And he'd spoken to no one but Falken.

Yet they were traced. Hiltonist Black Guards were busy now, destroying the last avenues of escape from Earth, avenues that he, Falken, had led them through.

But how? He knew he hadn't given himself away. For thirty years he'd been spiriting Unregenerates away from Gantry Hilton's strongholds of Peace and Happiness. He was too old a hand for blunders.

Yet, somehow, the Black Guards caught up with them at Losangles, where the *Falcon* lay hidden. And, somehow, they got away, with a starving green-eyed girl named Kitty....

"Not Kitty," Falken muttered. "Kitty's Happy. Hilton took Kitty, thirty years ago. On our wedding day."

A starving waif named Sheila Moore, who begged him for help, because he was Eric Falken and almost a god to the Unregenerates. They got away in the *Falcon*, but the Hiltonist ships followed.

Driven, hopeless flight, desperate effort to shake pursuit before he was too close to the Sun. Time and again, using precious fuel and accelerations that tried even his tough body, Falken thought he had escaped.

But they found him again. It was uncanny, the way they found him.

Now he couldn't run any more. At least he'd led the Hiltonists away from the pitiful starving holes where his people hid, on the outer planets and barren asteroids and dark derelict hulks floating far outside the traveled lanes.

And he'd kill himself before the Hiltonist psycho-search could pick his brain of information about the Unregenerates. Kill himself, if he could wake up.

He began to laugh, a drunken, ragged chuckle. He couldn't stop laughing. He clung to the panel edge and laughed until the tears ran down his scarred, dark face.

"Stop it," said Sheila Moore. "Stop it, Falken!"

"Can't. It's funny. We live in hell for thirty years, we Unregenerates, fighting Hiltonism. We're licked, now. We were before we started.

"Now I'm going to die so they can suffer hell a few weeks more. It's so damned funny!"

*

Sleep dragged at him. Sleep, urgent and powerful. So powerful that it seemed like an outside force gripping his mind. His hands relaxed on the panel edge.

"Falken," said Sheila Moore. "Eric Falken!"

Some steely thing in her voice lashed him erect again. She crouched on the shelf bunk against the wall, her feral green eyes blazing, her thin body taut in its torn green silk.

"You've got to get away, Falken. You've got to escape."

He had stopped laughing. "Why?" he asked dully.

"We need you, Falken. You're a legend, a hope we cling to. If you give up, what are we to go on?"

She rose and paced the narrow deck. Paul Avery watched her from the bunk on the opposite wall, his amber eyes dull with the deep weariness that slackened his broad young body.

Falken watched her, too. The terrible urge for sleep hammered at him, bowed his grey-shot, savage head, drew the strength from his lean muscles. But he watched Sheila Moore.

That was why he had risked his life, and Avery's, and broken Unregenerate law to save her, unknown and untested. She blazed, somehow. She stabbed his brain with the same cold fire he had felt after Kitty was taken from him.

"You've got to escape," she said. "We can't give up, yet."

Her voice was distant, her raw-gold hair a detached haze of light. Darkness crept on Falken's brain.

"How?" he whispered.

"I don't know...Falken!" She caught him with thin painful fingers. "They're driving you down on Mercury. Why not trick them? Why not go—beyond?"

He stared at her. Even he would never have thought of that. Beyond the orbit of Mercury there was only death.

Avery leaped to his feet. For a startled instant Falken's brain cleared, and he saw the trapped, wild terror in Avery's face.

"We'd die," said Avery hoarsely. "The heat...."

Sheila faced him. "We'll die anyway, unless you want Psycho-Change. Why not try it, Eric? Their instruments won't work close to the Sun. They may even be afraid to follow."

The wiry, febrile force of her beat at them. "Try, Eric. We have nothing to lose."

Paul Avery stared from one to the other of them and then to the red lights that were ships. Abruptly he sank down on the edge of his bunk and dropped his broad, fair head in his hands. Falken saw the cords like drawn harp-strings on the backs of them.

"I...can't," whispered Falken. The command to sleep was once more a vast shout in his brain. "I can't think."

"You must!" said Sheila. "If you sleep, we'll be taken. You won't be able to kill yourself. They'll pick your brain empty. Then they'll Hiltonize you with the Psycho-Adjuster.

"They'll blank your brain with electric impulses and then transmit a whole new memory-pattern, even shifting the thought-circuits so that you won't think the same way. They'll change your metabolism, your glandular balance, your pigmentation, your face, and your fingerprints."

He knew she was recounting these things deliberately, to force him to fight. But still the weak darkness shrouded him.

"Even your name will be gone," she said. "You'll be placid and lifeless, lazing your life away, just one of Hilton's cattle." She took a deep breath and added, "Like Kitty."

He caught her shoulders, then, grinding the thin bone of them. "How did you know?"

"That night, when you saw me, you said her name. Perhaps I made you think of her. I know how it feels, Eric. They took the boy I loved away from me."

He clung to her, the blue distant fire in his eyes taking life from the hot, green blaze of hers. There was iron in her. He could feel the spark and clash of it against his mind.

"Talk to me," he whispered. "Keep me awake. I'll try."

Waves of sleep clutched Falken with physical hands. But he turned to the control panel.

The bitter blaze of Mercury stabbed his bloodshot eyes. Red lights hemmed him in. He couldn't think. And then Sheila Moore began to talk. Standing behind him, her thin vital hands on his shoulders, telling him the story of Hiltonism.

"Gantry Hilton's Psycho-Adjuster was a good thing at first. Through the mapping and artificial blanking of brain-waves and the use of electro-hypnotism—the transmission of thought-patterns directly to the brain—it cured non-lesional insanity, neuroses, and criminal tendencies. Then, at the end of the Interplanetary War...."

Red lights closing in. How could he get past the Spaceguard battery? Sheila's voice fought back the darkness. Speed, that was what he needed. And more guts than he'd ever had to use in his life before. And luck.

"Keep talking, Sheila. Keep me awake."

"...Hilton boomed his discovery. The people were worn out with six years of struggle. They wanted Hiltonism, Peace and Happiness. The passion for escape from life drove them like lunatics."

He found the emergency lever and thrust it down. The last ounce of hoarded power slammed into the rocket tubes. The *Falcon* reared and staggered.

Then she shot straight for Mercury, with the thin high scream of tortured metal shivering along the cabin walls.

CHILD OF THE SUN

Spaceshells burst. They shook the *Falcon*, but they were far behind. The ring of red lights was falling away. Acceleration tore at Falken's body, but the web of sleep was loosening. Sheila's voice cried to him, the story of man's slavery.

The naked, hungry peaks of Mercury snarled at Falken. And then the guns of the Spaceguard post woke up.

"Talk, Sheila!" he cried. "Keep talking!"

"So Gantry Hilton made himself a sort of God, regulating the thoughts and emotions of his people. There is no opposition now, except for the Unregenerates, and we have no power. Humanity walks in a placid stupor. It cannot feel dissatisfaction, disloyalty, or the will to grow and change. It cannot fight, even morally.

"Gantry Hilton is a god. His son after him will be a god. And humanity is dying."

There was a strange, almost audible snap in Falken's brain. He felt a quick, terrible stab of hate that startled him because it seemed no part of himself. Then it was gone, and his mind was clear.

He was tired to exhaustion, but he could think, and fight.

Livid, flaming stars leaped and died around him. Racked plates screamed in agony. Falken's lean hands raced across the controls. He knew now what he was going to do.

Down, down, straight into the black, belching mouths of the guns, gambling that his sudden burst of speed would confuse the gunners, that the tiny speck of his ship hurtling bow-on would be hard to see against the star-flecked depths of space.

Falken's lips were white. Sheila's thin hands were a sharp unnoticed pain on his shoulders. Down, down....The peaks of Mercury almost grazed his hull.

A shell burst searingly, dead ahead. Blinded, dazed, Falken held his ship by sheer instinct. Thundering rockets fought the gravitational pull for a moment. Then he was through, and across.

Across Mercury, in free space, a speeding mote lost against the titanic fires of the Sun.

*

Falken turned. Paul Avery lay still in his bunk, but his golden eyes were wide, staring at Falken. They dropped to Sheila Moore, who had slipped exhausted to the floor, and came back to Falken—and stared and stared with a queer, stark look that Falken couldn't read.

Falken cut the rockets and locked the controls. Heat was already seeping through the hull. He looked through shaded ports at the vast and swollen Sun.

No man in the history of space travel had ventured so close before. He wondered how long they could stand the heat, and whether the hull could screen off the powerful radiations.

His brain, with all its knowledge of the Unregenerate camps, was safe for a time. Knowing the hopelessness of it, he smiled sardonically, wondering if sheer habit had taken the place of reason.

Then Sheila's bright head made him think of Kitty, and he knew that his tired body had betrayed him. He could never give up.

He went down beside Sheila. He took her hands and said:

"Thank you. Thank you, Sheila Moore."

And then, quite peacefully, he was asleep with his head in her lap.

*

The heat was a malignant, vampire presence. Eric Falken felt it even before he wakened. He was lying in Avery's bunk, and the sweat that ran from his body made a sticky pool under him.

Sheila lay across from him, eyes closed, raw-gold hair pushed back from her temples. The torn green silk of her dress clung damply. The starved thinness of her gave her a strange beauty, clear and brittle, like sculptured ice.

She'd lived in alleys and cellars, hiding from the Hiltonists, because she wouldn't be Happy. She was strong, that girl. Like an unwanted cat that simply wouldn't die.

Avery sat in the pilot's chair, watching through the shaded port. He swung around as Falken got up. The exhaustion was gone from his square young face, but his eyes were still veiled and strange. Falken couldn't read them, but he sensed fear.

He asked, "How long have I slept?"

Avery shrugged. "The chronometer stopped. A long time, though. Twenty hours, perhaps."

Falken went to the controls. "Better go back now. We'll swing wide of Mercury, and perhaps we can get through." He hoped their constant velocity hadn't carried them too far for their fuel.

Relief surged over Avery's face. "The size of that Sun," he said jerkily. "It's terrifying. I never felt...."

He broke off sharply. Something about his tone brought Sheila's eyes wide open.

Suddenly, the bell of the mass-detector began to ring, a wild insistent jangle.

"Meteor!" cried Falken and leaped for the visor screen. Then he froze, staring.

It was no meteor, rushing at them out of the vast blaze of the Sun. It was a planet.

A dark planet, black as the infinity behind it, barren and cruel as starvation, touched in its jagged peaks with subtle, phosphorescent fires.

Paul Avery whispered, "Good Lord! A planet, here? But it's impossible!"

Sheila Moore sprang up.

"No! Remember the old legends about Vulcan, the planet between Mercury and the Sun? Nobody believed in it, because they could never find it. But they could never explain Mercury's crazy orbit, either, except by the gravitational interference of another body."

Avery said, "Surely the Mercurian observatories would have found it?" A pulse began to beat in his strong white throat.

"It's there," snapped Falken impatiently. "And we'll crash it in a minute if we...Sheila! Sheila Moore!"

LEIGH BRACKETT

The dull glare from the ports caught the proud, bleak lines of his gypsy face, the sudden fire in his blue eyes.

"This is a world, Sheila! It might be a world for us, a world where Unregenerates could live, and wait!"

She gasped and stared at him, and Paul Avery said:

"Look at it, Falken! No one, nothing could live there."

Falken said softly, "Afraid to land and see?"

Yellow eyes burned into his, confused and wild. Then Avery turned jerkily away.

"No. But you can't land, Falken. Look at it."

Falken looked, using a powerful search-beam, probing. Vulcan was smaller even than Mercury. There was no atmosphere. Peaks like splinters of black glass bristled upward, revolving slowly in the Sun's tremendous blaze.

The beam went down into the bottomless dark of the canyons. There was nothing there, but the glassy rock and the dim glints of light through it.

"All the same," said Falken, "I'm going to land." If there was even a tiny chance, he couldn't let it slip.

Unregeneracy was almost dead in the inhabited worlds. Paul Avery was the only recruit in months. And it was dying in the miserable outer strongholds of independence.

Starvation, plague, cold, and darkness. Insecurity and danger, and the awful lost terror of humans torn from earth and light. Unless they could find a place of safety, with warmth and light and dirt to grow food in, where babies could be born and live, Gantry Hilton would soon have the whole Solar System for his toy.

There were no more protests. Falken set the ship down with infinite skill on a ledge on the night side. Then he turned, feeling the blood beat in his wrists and throat.

"Vac suits," he said. "There are two and a spare."

They got into them, shuffled through the airlock, and stood still, the first humans on an undiscovered world.

CHILD OF THE SUN

*

Lead weights in their boots held them so that they could walk. Falken thrust at the rock with a steel-shod alpenstock.

"It's like glass," he said. "Some unfamiliar compound, probably, fused out of raw force in the Solar disturbance that created the planets. That would explain its resistance to heat."

Radio headphones carried Avery's voice back to him clearly, and Falken realized that the stuff of the planet insulated against Solar waves, which would normally have blanketed communication.

"Whatever it is," said Avery, "it sucks up light. That's why it's never been seen. Only little glimmers seep through, too feeble for telescopes even on Mercury to pick up against the Sun. Its mass is too tiny for its transits to be visible, and it doesn't reflect."

"A sort of dark stranger, hiding in space," said Sheila, and shivered. "Look, Eric! Isn't that a cave mouth?"

Falken's heart gave a great leap of hope. There were caves on Pluto. Perhaps, in the hidden heart of this queer world....

They went toward the opening. It was surprisingly warm. Falken guessed that the black rock diffused the Sun's heat instead of stopping it.

Thin ragged spires reared overhead, stabbing at the stars. Furtive glints of light came and went in ebon depths. The cave opened before them, and their torches showed glistening walls dropping sheer away into blackness.

Falken uncoiled a thousand-foot length of synthetic fiber rope from his belt. It was no larger than a spider web, and strong enough to hold Falken and Avery together. He tied it to each of their metal boots to and let it down.

It floated endlessly out, the lead weight dropping slowly in the light gravity. Eight hundred, nine hundred feet. When there were five feet of rope left in Falken's hand it stopped.

"Well," he said. "There *is* a bottom."

Paul Avery caught his arm. "You aren't going down?"

"Why not?" Falken scowled at him, puzzled. "Stay here, if you prefer. Sheila?"

"I'm coming with you."

"All right," whispered Avery. "I'll come." His amber eyes were momentarily those of a lion caught in a pit. Afraid, and dangerous.

Dangerous? Falken shook his head irritably. He drove his alpenstock into a crack and made the rope fast.

"Hang onto it," he said. "We'll float like balloons, but be careful. I'll go first. If there's anything wrong down there, chuck off your other boot and climb up fast."

They went down, floating endlessly on the weighted rope. Little glints of light fled through the night-dark walls. It grew hot. Then Falken struck a jog in the cleft wall and felt himself sliding down a forty-five-degree offset. Abruptly, there was light.

Falken yelled, in sharp, wild warning.

The thing was almost on him. A colossus with burning eyes set on foot-long stalks, with fanged jaws agape and muscles straining.

Falken grabbed for his blaster. The quick motion overbalanced him. Sheila slid down on him and they fell slowly together, staring helplessly at destruction, charging at them through a rainbow swirl of light.

The creature rushed by, in utter silence.

Paul Avery landed, his blaster ready. Falken and Sheila scrambled up, cold with the sweat of terror.

"What was it?" gasped Sheila.

Falken said shakily, "God knows!" He turned to look at their surroundings.

And swept the others back into the shadow of the cleft.

Riders hunted the colossus. Riders of a shape so mad that even in madness no human could have conceived them. Riders on steeds like the arrowing tails of comets, hallooing on behind a pack of nightmare hounds....

CHILD OF THE SUN

Cold sweat drenched him. "How can they live without air?" he whispered. "And why didn't they see us?"

There was no answer. But they were safe, for the moment. The light, a shifting web of prismatic colors, showed nothing moving.

They stood on a floor of the glassy black rock. Above and on both sides walls curved away into the wild light—sunlight, apparently, splintered by the shell of the planet. Ahead there was a ebon plain, curving to match the curve of the vault.

Falken stared at it bitterly. There was no haven here. No life as he knew it could survive in this pit. Yet there was life, of some mad sort. Another time, they might not escape.

"Better go back," he said wearily, and turned to catch the rope.

The cleft was gone.

Smooth and unbroken, the black wall mocked him. Yet he hadn't moved more than two paces. He smothered a swift stab of fear.

"Look for it," he snapped. "It must be here."

But it wasn't. They searched, and came again together, to stare at each other with eyes already a little mad.

Paul Avery laughed sharply. "There's something here," he said. "Something alive."

Falken snarled, "Of course, you fool! Those creatures...."

"No. Something else. Something laughing at us."

"Shut up, Avery," said Sheila. "We can't go to pieces now."

"And we can't just stand here glaring." Falken looked out through the rainbow dazzle. "We may as well explore. Perhaps there's another way out."

Avery chuckled, without mirth. "And perhaps there isn't. Perhaps there was never a way in. What happened to it, Falken?"

"Control yourself," said Falken silkily, "or I'll rip off your oxygen valve. All right. Let's go."

They went a long way across the plain in the airless, unechoing silence, slipping on glassy rock, dazzled by the wheeling colors.

Then Falken saw the castle.

16

It loomed quite suddenly—a bulk of squat wings with queer, twisted turrets and straggling windows. Falken scowled. He was sure he hadn't seen it before. Perhaps the light....

They hesitated. Icy moth-wings flittered over Falken's skin. He would have gone around, but black walls seemed to stretch endlessly on either side of the castle.

"We go in," he said, and shuddered at the thought of meeting folk like those who hunted the flaming-eyed colossus.

Blasters ready, they went up flat titanic steps. A hall without doors stretched before them. They went down it.

*

Falken had a dizzy sense of *change*. The walls quivered as though with a wash of water over them. And then there were doors opening out of a round hall.

He opened one. There was a round hall beyond, with further doors. He turned back. The hall down which they had come had vanished. There were only doors. Hundreds of them, of odd shapes and sizes, like things imperfectly remembered.

Paul Avery began to laugh.

Falken struck him, hard, over the helmet. He stopped, and Sheila caught Falken's arm, pointing.

Shadows came, rushing and wheeling like monstrous birds. Cold dread caught Falken's heart. Shadows, hunting them....

He choked down the mad laughter rising in his own throat. He opened another door.

Halls, with doors. The shadows swept after them. Falken hurled the doors open, faster and faster, but there was never anything beyond but another hall, with doors.

His heart was gorged and painful. His clothing was cold on his sweating body. He plunged on and on through black halls and drifting shards of light, with the shadows dancing all around and doors, doors, doors.

CHILD OF THE SUN

Paul Avery made a little empty chuckle. "It's laughing," he mumbled and went down on the black floor. The shadows leaped.

Sheila's eyes were a staring fire in her starved white face. Her terror shocked against Falken's brain and steadied it.

"Take his feet," he said harshly. "Take his feet."

They staggered on with their burden. And presently there were no more doors, and no roof overhead. Only the light and the glassy walls, and the dancing shadows.

The walls were thin in places. Through them Falken saw the dark colossus with its flaming eyes, straining through the spangled light. After it came the hounds and hunters, not gaining nor falling back, riding in blind absorption.

The walls faded, and the shadows. They were alone in the center of the black plain. Falken looked back at the castle.

There was nothing but the flat and naked rock.

He laid Avery down. He saw Sheila Moore fall beside him. He laughed, one small, mad chuckle. Then he crouched beside the others, his scarred gypsy face a mask of living stone.

Whether it was then, or hours later that he heard the voice, Falken never knew. But it spoke loudly in his mind, that voice. It brought him up, his futile blaster raised.

"You are humans," said the voice. "How wonderful!"

Falken looked upward, sensing a change in the light.

Something floated overhead. A ten-foot area of curdled glory, a core of blinding brilliance set in a lacy froth of fire.

The beauty of it caught Falken's throat. It shimmered with a sparkling opalescence, infinitely lovely—a living, tender flame floating in the rainbow light. It caught his heart, too, with a deep sadness that drifted in dim, faded colors beneath the brilliant veil.

It said, clearly as a spoken voice in his mind:

"Yes. I live, and I speak to you."

Sheila and Avery had risen. They stared, wide-eyed, and Sheila whispered, "What are you?"

18

LEIGH BRACKETT

The fire-thing coiled within itself. Little snapping flames licked from its edges, and its colors laughed.

"A female, isn't it? Splendid! I shall devise something very special." Colors rippled as its thoughts changed. "You amaze me, humans. I cannot read your minds, beyond thoughts telepathetically directed at me, but I can sense their energy output.

"I had picked the yellow one for the strongest. He appeared to be so. Yet he failed, and you others fought through."

Avery stared at Falken with the dawn of an appalled realization in his amber eyes. Falken asked of the light:

"What are you?"

The floating fire dipped and swirled. Preening peacock tints rippled through it, to be drowned in fierce, proud scarlet. It said:

"I am a child of the Sun."

*

It watched them gape in stunned amazement, and laughed with mocking golden notes.

"I will tell you, humans. It will amuse me to have an audience not of my own creating. Watch!"

A slab of the glassy rock took form before them. Deep in it, a spot of brilliance grew.

It was a Sun, in the first blaze of its virile youth. It strode the path of its galactic orbit alone. Then, from the wheeling depths of space, a second Sun approached.

It was huge, burning with a blue-white radiance. There was a mating, and the nine worlds were born in a rush of supernal fire.

And there was life. Not on the nine burning planets. But in free space, little globes of fire, bits of the Sun itself shocked somehow to intelligence in the vast explosion of energy.

The picture blurred. The colors of the floating light were dulled and dreamy.

"There were many of us," it sighed. "We were like tiny Suns, living on the conversion of our own atoms. We played, in open space...."

CHILD OF THE SUN

Dim pictures washed the screen, glories beyond human comprehension—a faded vision of splendor, of alien worlds and the great wheeling Suns of outer space. The voice murmured:

"Like Suns, we radiated our energy. We could draw strength from our parent, but not enough. We died. But I was stronger than the rest, and more intelligent. I built myself a shell."

"Built it!" whispered Avery. "But how?"

"All matter is built of raw energy, electron and proton existing in a free state. With a part of my own mass I built this world around myself, to hold the energy of the Sun and check the radiation of my own vitality.

"I have lived, where my race died. I have watched the planets cool and live and die. I am not immortal. My mass grows less as it drains away through my shell. But it will be a long, long time. I shall watch the Sun die, too."

The voice was silent. The colors were ashes of light. Falken was stricken with a great poignant grief.

Then, presently, the little malicious flames frothed to life again, and the voice said:

"My greatest problem is amusement. Here in this black shell I am forced to devise pleasures from my own imagination."

Falken gasped. "The hunters, the cleft that vanished, and that hellish castle?" He was suddenly cold and hot at once.

"Clever, eh? I created my hunt some eons ago. According to my plan the beast can neither escape nor the hunters catch him. But, owing to the uncertainty factor, there is one chance in some hundreds of billions that one or the other event may occur. It affords me endless amusement."

"And the castle?" said Falken silkily. "That amused you, too."

"Oh, yes! Your emotional reactions....Most interesting!" Falken raised his blaster and fired at the core of the light.

Living fire coiled and writhed. The Sun-child laughed.

"Raw energy only feeds me. What, are there no questions?"

Falken's voice was almost gentle. "Do you think of nothing but amusement?"

Savage colors rippled against the dim, sad mauves. "What else is there, to fill the time?"

Time. Time since little frozen Pluto was incandescent gas.

"You closed the opening we came through," said Avery abruptly.

"Of course."

"But you'll open it again? You'll let us go?"

The tone of his voice betrayed him. Falken knew, and Sheila.

"No," said Sheila throatily. "It won't let us go. It'll keep us up here to play with, until we die."

Ugly dark reds washed the Sun-child. "Death!" it whispered. "My creatures exist until I bid them vanish. But death, true death—that would be a supreme amusement!"

*

A desperate, helpless rage gripped Falken. The vast empty vault mocked him with his dead hopes. It jeered at him with solid walls that were built and shifted like smoke by the power of this lovely, soulless flame.

Built, and shifted....

Sudden fire struck his brain. He stood rigid, stricken dumb by the sheer magnificence of his idea. He began to tremble, and the wild hope swelled in him until his veins were gorged and aching.

He said, with infinite care, "You can't create real living creatures, can you?"

"No," said the Sun-child. "I can build the chemicals of their bodies, but the vital spark eludes me. My creatures are simply toys activated by the electrical interplay of atoms. They think, in limited ways, and they feel crude emotions, but they do not live in the true sense."

"But you can build other things? Rocks, soil, water, air?"

"Of course. It would take a great deal of my strength, and it would weaken my shell, since I should have to break down part of the rock

21

to its primary particles and rebuild. But even that I could do, without serious loss."

There was silence. The blue distant fires flared in Falken's eyes. He saw the others staring at him. He saw the chances of failure bulk over him like black thunderheads, crowned with madness and death.

But his soul shivered in ecstasy at the thing that was in it.

The Sun-child said silkily, "Why should I do all this?"

"For amusement," whispered Falken. "The most colossal game you have ever had."

Brilliant colors flared. "Tell me, human!"

"I must make a bargain first."

"Why should I bargain? You're mine, to do with as I will."

"Quite. But we couldn't last very long. Why waste your imagination on the three of us when you might have thousands?"

Avery's amber eyes opened wide. A shocked incredulity slackened Sheila's rigid muscles. The voice cried:

"Thousands of humans to play with?"

The eager greed sickened Falken. Like a child wanting a bright toy—only the toys were human souls.

"Not until the bargain is made," he said.

"Well? What is the bargain? Quick!"

"Let us go, in return for the game which I shall tell you."

"I might lose you, and then have nothing."

"You can trust us," Falken insisted. He was shaking, and his nerves ached. "Listen. There are thousands of my people, living like hunted beasts in the deserts of the Solar System. They need a world, to survive at all. If you'll build them one in the heart of this planet, I'll bring them here.

"You wouldn't kill them. You'd let them live, to admire and praise you for saving them. It would amuse you just to watch them for some time. Then you could take one, once in a while, for a special game.

"I don't want to do this. But it's better that they should live that way than be destroyed."

"And better for you, too, eh?" The Sun-child swirled reflectively. "Breed men like cattle, always have a supply. It's a wonderful idea...."

"Then you'll do it?" Sweat dampened Falken's brow.

"Perhaps....Yes! Tell me, quickly, what you want!"

Falken swung to his stunned and unbelieving companions. He gripped an arm of each, painfully hard.

"Trust me. Trust me, for God's sake!" he whispered. Then, aloud, "Help me to tell it what we need."

There was a little laughing ripple of golden notes in the Sun-child's light, but Falken was watching Sheila's eyes. A flash of understanding crossed them, a glint of savage hope.

"Oxygen," she said. "Nitrogen, hydrogen, carbon dioxide...."

"And soil," said Falken. "Lime, iron, aluminum, silicon...."

*

They came to on a slope of raw, red earth, still wet from the rain. A range of low hills lifted in the distance against a strange black sky. Small tattered clouds drifted close above in the rainbow's light.

Falken got to his feet. As far as he could see there were rolling stretches of naked earth, flecked with brassy pools and little ruddy streams. He opened his helmet and breathed the warm wet air. He let the rich soil trickle through his fingers and thought of the Unregenerates in their frozen burrows.

He smiled, because there were tears in his hard blue eyes.

Sheila gave a little sobbing laugh and cried, "Eric, it's done!" Paul Avery lifted dark golden eyes to the hills, and was silent.

There was a laughing tremble of color in the air where the Sun-child floated. Small wicked flames drowned the sad, soft mauves. The Sun-child said:

"Look, Eric Falken. There, behind you."

Falken turned—and looked into his own face.

It stood there, his own lean body in the worn vac suit, his own gypsy face and the tangle of frosted curls. Only the eyes were

23

different. The chill, distant blue was right, but there were spiteful flecks of gold, a malicious sparkle that was like....

"Yes," purred the Sun-child. "Myself. A tiny particle, to activate the shell. A perfect likeness, no?"

A slow, creeping chill touched Falken's heart. "Why?" he asked.

"Long ago I learned the art of lying from men. I lied about reading minds. Your plan to trick me into building this world and then destroy me was plain on the instant of conception."

Laughing wicked colors coiled and spun.

"Oh, but I'm enjoying this! Not since I built my shell have I had such a game! Can you guess why I made your double?"

Falken's lips were tight with pain, his eyes savage with remorse at his own stupidity.

"It—he will go in my ship to bring my people here."

He knew that the Sun-child had picked his unwitting brain as cleanly as any Hiltonist psycho-search.

In sudden desperation he drew his blaster and shot at the mocking likeness. Before he tripped the trigger-stud a wall of ebon glass was raised between them. The blast-ray slid away in harmless fire and died, burned out.

The other Falken turned and strode away across the new land. Falken watched him out of sight, not moving nor speaking, because there was nothing to do, nothing to say.

The lovely wicked fire of the Sun-child faded suddenly.

"I am tired," it said. "I shall suckle the Sun, and rest."

It floated away. For all his agony, Falken felt the heart-stab of its sad, dim colors. It faded like a wisp of lonely smoke into the splintered light.

Presently there was a blinding flash and a sharp surge of air as a fissure was opened. Falken saw the creature, far away, pressed to the roof of the vault and pulsing as it drank the raw blaze of the Sun.

"Oh, God," whispered Falken. "Oh, God, what have I done?"

Falken laughed, one harsh wild cry. Then he stood quite still, his hands at his sides, his face a mask cut deep in dark stone.

"Eric," whispered Sheila. "Please. I can't be brave for you all the time."

He was ashamed of himself then. He shook the black despair away with cynical fatalism.

"All right, Sheila. We'll be heroes to the bitter end. You, Avery. Get your great brain working. How can we save our people, and, incidentally, our own skins?"

Avery flinched as though some swift fear had stabbed him. "Don't ask me, Falken. Don't!"

"Why not? What the devil's the matter...." Falken broke off sharply. Something cold and fierce and terrifying came into his face. "Just a minute, Avery," he said gently. "Does that mean you think you know a way?"

"I....For God's sake, let me alone!"

"You do know a way," said Falken inexorably. "Why shouldn't I ask you, Paul Avery? Why shouldn't you try to save your people?"

Golden eyes met his, desperate, defiant, bewildered, and pitiful all at once.

"They're not my people," whispered Avery.

They were caught, then, in a strange silence. Soundless wheeling rainbows brushed the new earth, glimmered in the brassy pools. Far up on the black crystal of the vault the Sun-child pulsed and breathed. And there was stillness, like the morning of creation.

Eric Falken took one slow, taut step, and said, "Who are you?"

The answer whispered across the raw red earth.

"Miner Hilton, the son of Gantry."

*

Falken raised the blaster, forgotten in his hand. Miner Hilton, who had been Paul Avery, looked at it and then at Falken's face, a shield of dark iron over cold, terrible flame.

He shivered, but he didn't move, nor speak.

CHILD OF THE SUN

"You know a way to fight that thing," said Falken, very softly, in his throat. "I want to kill you. But you know a way."

"I—I don't know. I can't...." Golden tortured eyes went to Sheila Moore and stayed there, with a dreadful lost intensity.

Falken's white teeth showed. "You want to tell, Miner Hilton. You want to help us, don't you? Because of Sheila!"

Young Hilton's face flamed red, and then went white. Sheila cried sharply,

"Eric, don't! Can't you see he's suffering?"

But Falken remembered Kitty, and the babies who were born and died on freezing rock, without sun or shelter. He said,

"She'd never have you, Hilton. And I'll tell you this. Perhaps I can't force out of you what you know. But if I can't, I swear to God I'll kill you with my own hands."

He threw back his head and laughed suddenly. "Gantry Hilton's son—in love with an Unregenerate!"

"Wait, Eric." Sheila Moore put a hand on his arm to stop him, and went forward. She took Miner Hilton by the shoulders and looked up at him, and said,

"It isn't so impossible, Miner Hilton. Not if what I think is true."

Falken stared at her in stunned amazement, beyond speech or movement. Then his heart was torn with sudden pain, and he knew, with the clarity of utter truth, that he loved Sheila Moore.

She said to Miner Hilton, "Why did you do this? And how?"

Young Hilton's voice was flat and strained. He made a move as though to take her hands from his shoulders, but he didn't. He stared across her red-gold head, at Falken.

"Something had to be done to stamp out the Unregenerates. They're a barrier to complete peace, a constant trouble. Eric Falken is their god, as—as Sheila said. If we could trap him, the rest would be easy. We could cure his people.

"My father couldn't do it himself. He's old, and too well-known. He sent me, because mine is the only other brain that could stand what I had to do. My father has trained me well.

"To get me by the psycho-search, my father gave me a temporary brain pattern. After I was accepted as a refugee, I established mental contact with him...."

"Mental contact," breathed Falken. "That was it. That's why you were always so tired, why I couldn't shake pursuit."

"Go on," said Sheila, with a queer gentleness.

Hilton stared into space, without seeing.

"I almost had you in Losangles, Falken, but you were too quick for the Guards. Then, when we were trapped at Mercury, I tried to make you sleep. I was leading those ships, too.

"But I was tired, and you fought too well, you and Sheila. After that we were too close to the Sun. My thought waves wouldn't carry back to the ships."

He looked at Falken, and then down at Sheila's thin face.

"I didn't know there were people like you," he whispered. "I didn't know men could feel things, and fight for them like that. In my world, no one wants anything, no one fights, or tries....And I have no strength. I'm afraid."

Sheila's green eyes caught his, compelled them.

"Leave that world," she said. "You see it's wrong. Help us to make it right again."

In that second, Falken saw what she was doing. He was filled with admiration, and joy that she didn't really care for Hilton—and then doubt, that perhaps she did.

Miner Hilton closed his eyes. He struck her hands suddenly away and stepped back, and his blaster came ready into his hand.

"I can't," he whispered. His lips were white. "My father has taught me. He trusts me. And I believe in him. I must!"

Hilton looked where the glow of the Sun-child pulsed against ebon rock. "The Unregenerates won't trouble us any more."

CHILD OF THE SUN

He raised the muzzle of his blaster to his head.

*

It was then that Falken remembered his was empty. He dropped it and sprang. He shocked hard against Hilton's middle, struck him down, clawing for his gun arm. But Hilton was heavy, and strong.

He rolled away and brought his barrel lashing down across Falken's temple. Falken crouched, dazed and bleeding, in the mud.

He laughed, and said, "Why don't you kill me, Hilton?"

Hilton looked from Falken's uncowed, snarling face to Sheila. The blaster slipped suddenly from his fingers. He covered his face with his hands and was silent, shivering.

Falken said, with curious gentleness, "That proves it. You've got to have faith in a thing, to kill or die for it."

Hilton whispered, "Sheila!" She smiled and kissed him, and Falken looked steadfastly away, wiping the blood out of his eyes.

Hilton grasped suddenly at the helmet of his vac-suit. He talked, rapidly, as he worked.

"The Sun-child creates with the force of its mind. It understands telekinesis, the control of the basic electrical force of the universe by thought, just as the wise men of our earth understood it. The men who walked on the water, and moved mountains, and healed the sick.

"We can only attack it through its mind. We'll try to weaken its thought-force, destroy anything it sends against us."

His fingers flashed between the helmet radio and the repair kit which is a part of every vac suit, using wires, spare parts, tools.

"There," said Hilton, after a long time. "Now yours."

Falken gave him his helmet. "Won't the Sun-child know what we're doing?" he asked, rather harshly.

Hilton shook his fair head. "It's weak now. It won't think about us until it has fed. Perhaps two hours more."

"Can you read its thoughts?" demanded Falken sourly.

"A very little," said Hilton, and Sheila laughed, quietly.

Hilton worked feverishly. Falken watched his deft fingers weaving a bewildering web of wires between the three helmets, watched him shift and change, tune and adjust. He watched the sun-child throb and sparkle as the strength of the Sun sank into it. He watched Sheila Moore, staring at Hilton with eyes of brilliant green.

He never knew how much time passed. Only that the Sun-child gave a little rippling sigh of light and floated down. The fissure closed above it. Sheila caught her breath, sharp between her teeth.

Hilton rose. He said rapidly.

"I've done the best I can. It's crude, but the batteries are strong. The helmets will pick up and amplify the energy-impulses of our brains. We'll broadcast a single negative impulse, opposed to every desire the Sun-thing has.

"Stay close together, because if the wires are broken between the helmets we lose power, and it's going to take all the strength we have to beat that creature."

Falken put on his helmet. Little copper discs, cut from the sheet in the repair kit and soldered to wires with Hilton's blaster, fitted to his temples. Through the vision ports he could see the web of wires that ran from the three helmets through a maze of spare grids and a condenser, and then into the slender shaft of a crude directional antenna.

Hilton said, "Concentrate on the single negative, *No*."

Falken looked at the lovely shimmering cloud, coming toward them.

"It won't be easy," he said grimly, "to concentrate."

Sheila's eyes were savage and feral, watching that foam of living flame. Hilton's face was hidden. He said,

"Switch on your radios."

Power hummed from the batteries. Falken felt a queer tingle in his brain.

CHILD OF THE SUN

The Sun-child hovered over them. Its mind-voice was silent, and Falken knew that the electrical current in his helmet was blanking his own thoughts.

They linked arms. Falken set his brain to beating out an impulse, like a radio signal, opposing the negative of his mind to the positive of the Sun-child's.

*

Falken stood with the others on spongy, yielding soil. Dim plant-shapes rose on all sides as far as he could see, forming an impenetrable tangle of queer geometric shapes that made him reel with a sense of spatial distortion.

Overhead, in a sea-green sky, three tiny suns wheeled in mad orbits about a common center. There was a smell in the air, a rotting stench that was neither animal or vegetable.

Falken stood still, pouring all his strength into that single mental command to stop.

The tangled geometric trees wavered momentarily. Dizzily, through the wheeling triple suns, the Sun-child showed, stabbed through with puzzled, angry scarlet.

The landscape steadied again. And the ground began to move.

It crawled in small hungry wavelets about Falken's feet. The musky, rotten smell was heavy as oil. Sheila and Hilton seemed distant and unreal, their faces hidden in the helmets.

Falken gripped them together and drove his brain to its task. He knew what this was. The reproduction of another world, remembered from the Sun-child's youth. If they could only stand still, and not think about it....

He felt the earth lurch upward, and guessed that the Sun-child had raised its creation off the floor of the cavern.

The earth began to coil away from under his feet.

*

For a giddy instant Falken saw the true world far below, and the Sun-child floating in rainbow light.

It was angry. He could tell that from its color. Then suddenly the anger was drowned in a swirl of golden motes.

It was laughing. The Sun-child was laughing.

Falken fought down a sharp despair. A terrible fear of falling oppressed him. He heard Sheila scream. The world closed in again.

Sheila Moore looked at him from between two writhing trees.

He hadn't felt her go. But she was there. Hairy branches coiled around her, tore her vac-suit. She shrieked....

Falken cried out and went forward. Something held him. He fought it off, driven by the agony in Sheila's cry.

Something snapped thinly. There was a flaring shock inside his helmet. He fell, and staggered up and on, and the hungry branches whipped away from the girl.

She stood there, her thin white body showing through the torn vac-suit, and laughed at him.

He saw Miner Hilton crawling dazed on the living ground, toward the thing that looked like Sheila and laughed with mocking golden motes in its eyes.

A vast darkness settled on Falken's soul. He turned. Sheila Moore crouched where he had thrown her from him, in his struggle to help the lying shell among the trees.

He went and picked her up. He said to Miner Hilton,

"Can we fix these broken wires?"

Hilton shook his head. The shock of the breaking seemed to have steadied him a little. "No," he said. "Too much burned out."

"Then we're beaten." Falken turned a bitter, snarling face to the green sky, raised one futile fist and shook it. Then he was silent, looking at the others.

Sheila Moore said softly, "This is the end, isn't it?"

Falken nodded. And Miner Hilton said,

"I'm not afraid, now." He looked at the trees that hung over them, waiting, and shook his head. "I don't understand. Now that I know I'm going to die, I'm not afraid."

CHILD OF THE SUN

Sheila's green eyes were soft and misty. She kissed Hilton, slowly and tenderly, on the lips.

Falken turned his back and stared at the twisted ugly trees. He didn't see them. And he wasn't thinking of the Unregenerates and the world he'd won and then lost.

*

Sheila's hand touched him. She whispered, "Eric...."

Her eyes were deep, glorious green. Her pale starved face had the brittle beauty of wind-carved snow. She held up her arms and smiled.

Falken took her and buried his gypsy face in the raw gold of her hair.

"How did you know?" he whispered. "How did you know I loved you?"

"I just—knew."

"And Hilton?"

"He doesn't love me, Eric. He loves what I stand for. And anyway...I can say this now, because we're going to die. I've loved you since I first saw you. I love you more than Tom, and I'd have died for him."

Hungry tree branches reached for them, barely too short. Buds were shooting up underfoot. But Falken forgot them, the alien life and the wheeling suns that were only a monstrous dream, and the Sun-child who dreamed them.

For that single instant he was happy, as he had not been since Kitty was lost.

Presently he turned and smiled at Hilton, and the wolf look was gone from his face. Hilton said quietly.

"Maybe she's right, about me. I don't know. There's so much I don't know. I'm sorry I'm not going to live to find out."

"We're all sorry," said Falken, "about not living." A sudden sharp flare lighted his eyes. "Wait a minute!" he whispered. "There may be a chance...."

32

He was taut and quivering with terrible urgency, and the buds grew and yearned upward around their feet.

"You said we could only attack it through its mind. But there may be another way. Its memories, its pride...."

He raised his scarred gypsy face to the green sky and shouted,

"You, Child of the Sun! Listen to me! You have beaten us. Go ahead and kill us. But remember this. You're a child of the Sun, and we're only puny humans, little ground-crawlers, shackled with weakness and fear.

"But we're greater than you! Always and forever, greater than you!"

The writhing trees paused, the buds faltered in their hungry growth. Faintly, very faintly, the landscape flickered. Falken's voice rose to a ringing shout.

"You were a child of the Sun. You had the galaxy for a toy, all the vast depths of space to play in. And what did you do? You sealed yourself like a craven into a black tomb, and lost all your greatness in the whimsies of a wicked child.

"You were afraid of your destiny. You were too weak for your own strength. We fought you, we little humans, and our strength was so great that you had to beat us by a lying trick.

"You can read our minds, Sun-child. Read them. See whether we fear you. And see whether we respect you, you who boast of your parentage and dream dreams of lost glory, and hide in a dark hole like a frightened rat!"

*

For one terrible moment the alien world was suffused with a glare of scarlet—anger so great that it was almost tangible. Then it greyed and faded, and Falken could see Sheila's face, calm and smiling, and Hilton's fingers locked in hers.

The ground dropped suddenly. Blurred trees writhed against a fading sky, and the suns went out in ebon shadow. Falken felt clean earth under him. The rotting stench was gone.

CHILD OF THE SUN

He looked up. The Sun-child floated overhead, under the rocky vault. They were back in the cavern world.

The Sun-child's voice spoke in his brain, and its fires were a smoldering, dusky crimson.

"What was that you said, human?"

"Look into my mind and read it. You've thrown away your greatness. We had little, compared to you, but we kept it. You've won, but your very winning is a shame to you, that a child of the Sun should stoop to fight with little men."

The smoldering crimson burned and grew, into glorious wicked fire that was sheer fury made visible. Falken felt death coiling to strike him out of that fire. But he faced it with bitter, mocking eyes, and he was surprised, even then, that he wasn't afraid.

And the raging crimson fire faded and greyed, was quenched to a trembling mist of sad, dim mauves.

"You are right," whispered the Sun-child. "And I am shamed."

The ashes of burned-out flame stirred briefly. "I think I began to realize that when you fought me so well. You, Falken, who let your love betray you, and then shook your fist at me. I could kill you, but I couldn't break you. You made me remember...."

Deep in the core of the Sun-child there was a flash of the old proud scarlet.

"I am a child of the Sun, with the galaxy to play with. I have so nearly forgotten. I have tried to forget, because I knew that what I did was weak and shameful and craven. But you haven't let me forget, Falken. You've forced me to see, and know.

"You have made me remember. Remember! I am very old. I shall die soon, in open space. But I wish to see the Sun unveiled, and play again among the stars. The hunger has torn me for eons, but I was afraid. Afraid of death!

"Take this world, in payment for the pain I caused you. My creature will return here in Falken's ship and vanish on the instant of landing. And now...."

The scarlet fire burned and writhed. Shafts of joyous gold pierced through it. The Sun-child trembled, and its little foaming flames, were sheer glory, the hearts of Sun-born opals.

It rose in the rainbow air, higher and higher, rushing in a cloud of living light toward the black crystal of the vault.

Once more there was a blinding flash and a quick sharp rush of air. Faintly, in Falken's mind, a voice said,

"Thank you, human! Thank you for waking me from a dying sleep!"

A last wild shout of color on the air. And then it was gone, into open space and the naked fire of the Sun, and the rocky roof was whole.

Three silent people stood on the raw red earth of a new world.

www.ingramcontent.com/pod-product-compliance
Lightning Source LLC
Chambersburg PA
CBHW021005150626
46549CB00012BA/1345